The Sea Hole

For my Mum and Dad

First published in 1997 by Macmillan Children's Books
a division of Macmillan Publishers Limited
25 Eccleston Place, London SW1W 9NF
and Basingstoke
Associated companies worldwide

ISBN 0 333 64644 4 (hardback)
ISBN 0 333 67444 8 (paperback)

1 3 5 7 9 8 6 4 2

A CIP catalogue record for this book is available
from the British Library

Printed in Hong Kong

The Sea Hole

R.S.N.C

Ross Collins

Macmillan Children's Books

"Look at the sea, Ben," said Dad. "Don't you think it's a bit like a huge skin?"

Ben looked confused, so his Dad went on. "The sea covers three quarters of the world, you know, always moving and repairing itself, if it needs it."

Ben was still puzzled. Dad tried to explain. "When the waves rush forward too fast they make holes in the sea. That's why they move back quickly, to close them up again."

Ben watched the tide as the evening light bounced off the waves. A sea skin was a nice idea, thought Ben, but Dad had also told him that Italians had blue teeth and that Aunt Margaret came from Mars.

Dad stood up.

"Time to go home," he said, "or you'll catch cold."

Ben's dad was a fisherman, which was lucky, because Ben was an expert fish-eater. Sole, haddock, halibut, plaice – Ben ate the lot.

Sometimes Dad would have to go to sea for days at a time to catch enough fish because, he said, Ben ate so much. Ben missed his Dad, but filled his days playing on the shore with his fat dog, Belly, or helping to sew up holes in the fishing nets.

Winter arrived, closely followed by a cold for Ben. He didn't like being stuck inside all day, and Belly didn't like having no one to play with.

Winter brought the storms, too. The boats couldn't go out and Dad had to stay at home. Ben liked having Dad around more often, but Dad worried about not catching any fish.

This year the storms seemed worse than usual.

"You had better hurry up and get better, Ben," he said. "Look what you've made the sea do."

Ben sniffed.

Soon things started to happen that were even stranger than Ben's father's stories.

All the fishermen were bewildered.

"The last time the water was this wild," said one, "was the Great Storm of '37." "No, you old fool," said another, "surely it was the Typhoons of '42?"

"Ach, the flood of '76 was far worse than all those," grumbled a third.

Sometimes, if the night's flooding was particularly bad, people would wake up with new neighbours.

Some folk didn't like their old neighbours anyway and were glad for the change, but everybody agreed that something had to be done.

Night after night, as Ben lay in bed, he could hear the fishermen arguing over "plans of immediate action".

His ears red from listening, Ben decided that he would just have to find out what the sea wanted himself.

He wrapped up warm and, with Belly following, crept out of the house to set his little boat onto the billowy sea. Once all necessary supplies were aboard (one flask of soup), the pair sailed off into the night.

The sea seemed to know where it was
taking them and carried the little boat
further and further away from land.
　As they sailed, frightened fish tried to
jump into the boat to escape their unhappy
home. Ben got fed up with throwing them back,
and decided he wasn't so keen on fish any more.
　Suddenly the fish disappeared and Ben felt they
must be close. Then, in the distance, he saw it . . .

. . . and a BIG one at that.
A hole so huge that the sea
couldn't repair it.
"We'll have to fix it!" shouted Ben.
Belly did not look happy at all.

Ben had to think quickly. The sea was far too chilly for him, what with his cold and all. Belly, however, was a surprisingly good swimmer for such a tubby dog. Ben tied a long piece of shipping rope firmly round Belly's belly and held tight as the little dog jumped courageously into the icy water.

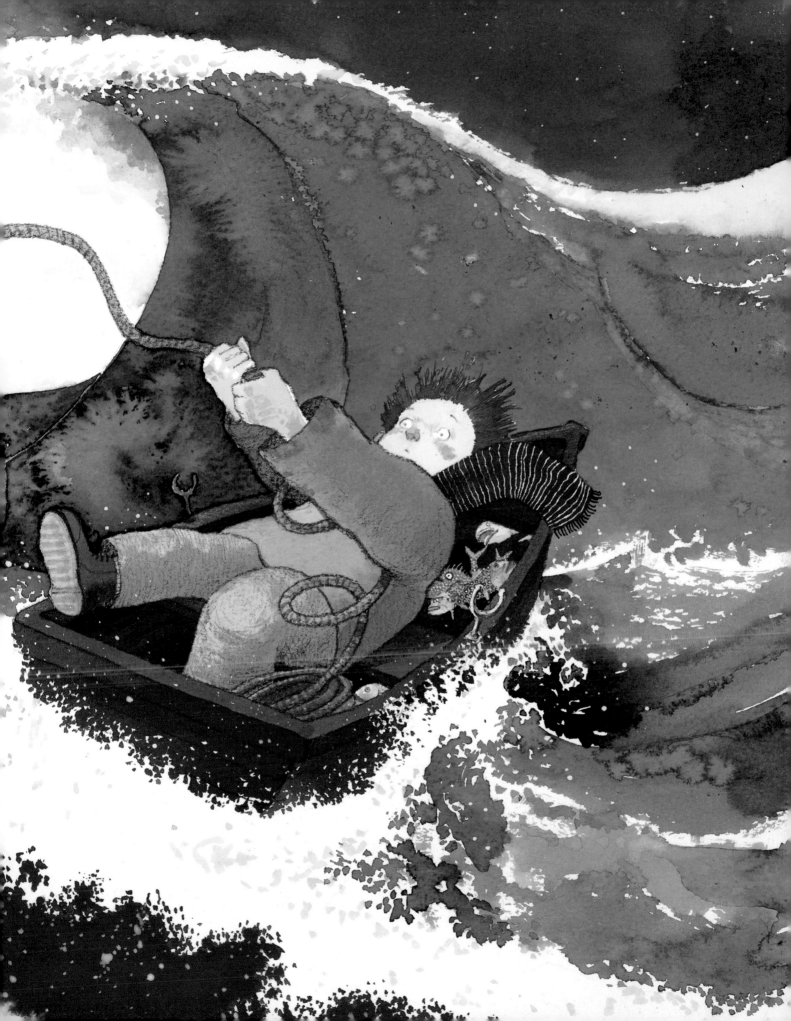

Belly knew what to do and slowly began to swim and jump back and forth, back and forth across the hole in the sea.

Once Belly had finished and Ben had pulled the soaking
dog to safety, they began to heave on the rope. They
tugged and tugged until slowly the sides of the hole began
to edge closer together. Ben thought it would never close,
but finally, with one last heave there was a . . .

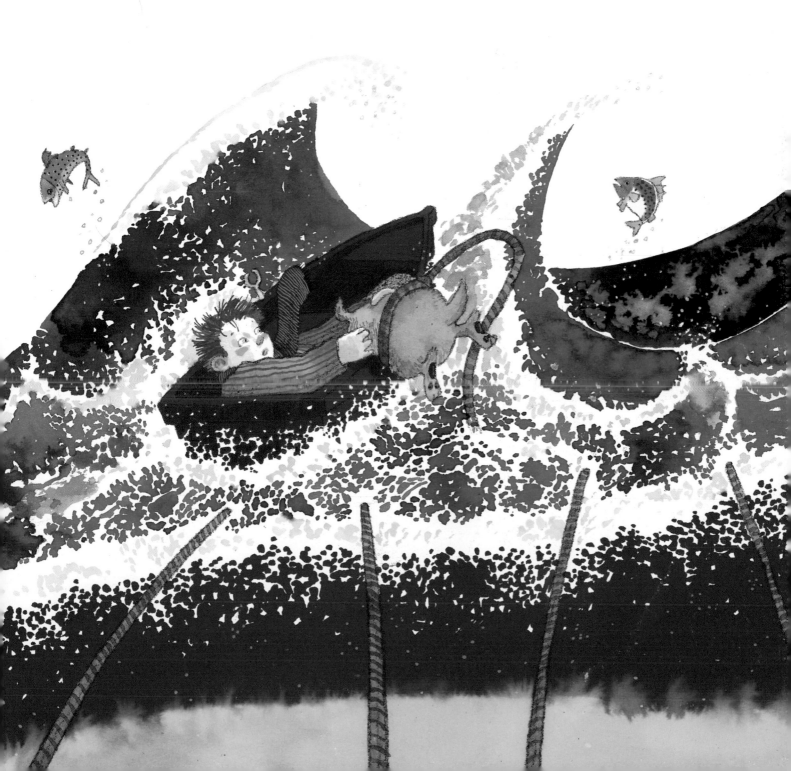

Splash!

. . . and the hole was gone.
With a happy roar the sea
was calm again.

Ben found that his cold was
gone, too, and the morning
sun warmed them as they
drifted home on a happy tide.

When Ben's worried father found the pair, Ben was exhausted,
but had a story to tell even more amazing than one of his Dad's.

FALKIRK COUNCIL
LIBRARY SUPPORT
FOR SCHOOLS